Treasure Island

Retold from the Robert Louis Stevenson
original by Chris Tait

Illustrated by Lucy Corvino

STERLING CHILDREN'S BOOKS
New York

STERLING CHILDREN'S BOOKS
New York

An Imprint of Sterling Publishing Co., Inc.
1166 Avenue of the Americas
New York, NY 10036

ISBN 978-1-4027-9462-9

Library of Congress Cataloging-in-Publication Data
Tait, Chris.
    Treasure Island / abridged by Chris Tait; illustrated by Lucy Corvino; retold from the original
author, Robert Louis Stevenson.
        p. cm.—(Classic starts)
    Summary: While going through the possessions of a deceased guest who owed them money,
the mistress of the inn and her son find a treasure map that leads to a pirate fortune as well as
great danger.
    ISBN 1-4027-1318-5
    [1. Buried treasure—Fiction. 2. Pirates—Fiction. 3. Adventure and adventurers—Fiction.] I.
Corvino, Lucy, ill. II. Stevenson, Robert Louis. Treasure Island. III. Title. IV. Series.
PZ7.T1289Tr 2004
[Fic]—dc22

                                                                    2004014666

Distributed in Canada by Sterling Publishing Co., Inc.
c/o Canadian Manda Group, 664 Annette Street
Toronto, Ontario M6S 2C8, Canada
Distributed in the United Kingdom by GMC Distribution Services
Castle Place, 166 High Street, Lewes, East Sussex BN7 1XU, England
Distributed in Australia by NewSouth Books
University of New South Wales, Sydney, NSW 2052, Australia

For information about custom editions, special sales, and premium and corporate purchases,
please contact Sterling Special Sales at 800-805-5489 or specialsales@sterlingpublishing.com.

Manufactured in Canada

Lot#:
2 4 6 8 10 9 7 5 3 1
03/19

sterlingpublishing.com

Design by Renato Stanisic
Cover illustration by Lucy Corvino

CONTENTS

⌒

CHAPTER 1

The Old Sea Dog at the Admiral Benbow

A great number of people have asked me to write down the whole story of Treasure Island, and that I shall do. But I will leave out the location of the island, because the treasure is still out there. The story begins back when my father was running an inn called the Admiral Benbow. The night was bitter, and we could hear a howling wind outside when the old seaman with a scarred face first made his way through our door.

In he blew, a strange sight with his sea chest being dragged behind him in a wheelbarrow. He

was strong and tall, with nut-brown skin and a blackened pigtail hanging over a dirty blue coat. In fact, everything about him looked dirty, including his hands and nails. The whiteness of the scar that spread across his cheek stood out against his grimy skin. He whistled and sang a song I would hear many times:

"Fifteen men on a dead man's chest . . .
Yo-ho-ho, and a bottle of rum!"

After the man rapped his heavy stick on the floor, my father appeared. Our guest seemed not to notice him at first, so busy was he at looking around our inn.

"A handy cove," he said, "and convenient too. Been busy lately, have you?"

"No," my father answered, and that was the truth. Business had been slow.

"Well, then," he said, "this fine place will do

for me. Hey you there," he said to the man who pushed the barrow, "I'll want some help getting my chest upstairs. I'll stay down here a bit." He went on in a gruff tone. "I'm a plain man; bacon and eggs is what I want—and that view up there to watch for ships. You'll call me Captain."

He noticed my father's doubting look and threw down some gold coins, which he'd taken out of a small leather pouch. "You let me know," he said fiercely, "when I've worked through that! There's more where that came from!"

Though he looked shabby and his manners were coarse, he seemed used to being obeyed. The man who carried his things told us that he had just come into port that morning and that he had asked for a quiet inn along the coast. That was all we could learn about our mysterious guest.

He was a silent man who spent his days upon the cliffs looking through a shiny brass telescope out across the horizon. At night he would sit by the fire in our parlor. He would often not speak when spoken to and just as suddenly would blow his nose like a foghorn. Our guests kept their distance from him, as did I and my father.

After his evening stroll, he would ask whether any sailors had come along the road. At first we thought he was lonely, but soon we realized that he was hiding from someone. When a seaman did come by, he would watch through the curtains and be silent as a mouse.

He started to take me into his confidence. One day, he promised me a silver fourpenny a month if I would watch, with my "weather eye," for a one-legged sailor, and let him know if he appeared. He would sometimes scowl when I asked for payment, but would soon give in, knowing it was more important that I keep a lookout for him than to hold back my pay. "Keep a sharp lookout," he repeated, "for the one-legged man!"

This one-legged mystery man haunted my dreams, and on stormy nights, I would see him take shape in a nightmare. With his leg off at the knee, then at the hip, then as a monster with a leg in the middle of his body! He ran through my dreams, chasing me over fences and across fields. I was paying dearly for my helping him!

And though I feared this man, I was less afraid of the Captain than most. They cowered as he sang his wicked, wild sea songs. On stormy nights, he would tell terrible stories and urge us all to sing his chorus of "Yo-ho-ho, and a bottle of rum," the guests joining in for fear of their lives. He glared and slapped his hand on the table, flying into rages whenever the mood was upon him. None dared leave the table until he had finished his singing and storytelling and had reeled off to sleep.

And they were truly scary stories. Dreadful tales of hanging, plank walking, and storms at sea. He delighted in telling us that he had lived among the wickedest men who ever called themselves sailors, and his rough language shocked us as much as the crimes he spoke of.

My father thought the inn would be ruined. People would stay away, he said. But I think the Captain's presence brought newcomers to our inn. They were afraid at first, but they soon allowed some excitement to enter into their quiet lives—there was even a party in his honor where the young men called him "sea dog" and "old salt," and claimed he was the sort of fellow who made other nations show respect for us at sea.

But he stayed on long after his money had been spent, and that started to bother us. My father just never had enough courage to insist on more. If he mentioned it, the Captain roared at him and stared my father down until he left the room. I'm sure that was one reason my father became so ill.

The Captain never changed his clothes, and

when his hat frayed, he threw it into the sea. He repaired his own coat, and by the end of his stay, it was nothing but patches. He had no visitors, neither wrote nor received any letters, and spoke to the neighbors only when he was bored. None of us ever saw the great sea chest when it was open.

He was only challenged once, when Dr. Livesey came to check on my poor father. During a break, the doctor was having his dinner and speaking to another guest in the parlor while he waited for his horse. I followed him in and compared his neat appearance with that of the Captain: his coat seemed so clean, his manner so bright next to that of our filthy old pirate.

Suddenly, the Captain struck up his song:

"Fifteen men on a dead man's chest . . .
Yo-ho-ho, and a bottle of rum.
Drink and the Devil had done for the rest . . .
Yo-ho-ho, and a bottle of rum!"

I thought this chest was referring to his sea chest, and it got tangled in my dreams with the terrible one-legged monster of a man. But by now we had all stopped paying any attention to that song. It was only new to Dr. Livesey, who looked quite angrily at the Captain before going on with his conversation. Soon, the Captain waved his hand for silence and we all stopped talking, except for the good doctor, who went on speaking loud and clear. The Captain glared at him and commanded —"Silence belowdecks!" Dr. Livesey turned to him and said one thing—"I have never before found the need to listen to scoundrels, and I certainly shall not make any exceptions to-night!"

The Captain jumped up in an awful temper and flicked open his knife, threatening to stab the doctor. Dr. Livesey stood stock still and spoke in the same voice, loudly, saying—"If you do not put that knife away, I shall see you hang!" They glared at each other with terrible eyes, but the Captain soon folded and sat, growling like an old dog. But the doctor was not finished. "Now that I know your kind is in my district, know also that I'll have my eye on you. I'm not only a doctor. I'm also a judge. Let me hear one word of complaint against you, and I'll have you hunted down and driven out of town. Let that be warning enough to you!"

The doctor's horse soon came and he rode away. But the Captain held his peace that evening and for many more to come.

CHAPTER 2

Black Dog

Not long after, something mysterious occurred that rid us of the Captain, though not of his affairs. That winter was severe, and it was clear my father would not live to see the spring. He grew worse every day, and the inn was left to my mother and me to look after—our hands were too full to worry about our unpleasant guest.

One cold January morning, with a layer of frost on the cove and the sun still low, the Captain rose earlier than usual. With glass in hand and hat tilted back, he trudged down the beach, his rusty sword swinging under his old blue coat. He strode along, snorting, as if still insulted by Dr. Livesey.

Mother was upstairs with Father and I was setting the table when the door opened and a pale, waxy man with two missing fingers appeared. I had been keeping an eye out for a man with one leg and here was one who, though he didn't seem like a sailor, had something of the sea about him.

I asked what he wanted. He sat down and motioned for me to come near.

"Is this here table for my pal, Bill?" he asked, leering.

I told him I knew no Bill but that the table was for a man we called the Captain.

"Well," he said, "old Bill would want to be called Captain. Has a deepish cut on his right cheek and a funny way about him. Now, is my boy Bill in this here house today?"

I told him he was out walking, and he demanded to know where. When I told him, he stood up and made a mock salute. I didn't know what to do. This fellow had a strange manner and he waited behind the door like a cat for a mouse. Soon enough, we saw the Captain approach.

"Now," he said, "let's give Bill a little surprise." Saying this, he hid us both behind the door. I could tell he, too, was scared—his heavy breathing gave him away. He loosened his sword and stood ready. When the Captain marched through, heading for his breakfast, the stranger called out, trying to sound brave.

"Bill!"

The Captain turned as if he had seen a ghost.

"Black Dog!" he gasped.

"Who else?" asked the thin man. "Ah," he said, "we've seen many good years since I lost these two claws . . ." And with that he held up his terrible hand.

"Well," said the Captain bluntly, "you found me—now what is it you want?"

The thin man then sent me away. I listened as well as I could to get the sense of their rude talk.

Suddenly they started yelling—the chair and table went over and the Captain with his drawn sword was chasing Black Dog, who started bleeding from his shoulder. The Captain swung again and put a notch in the sign over our door that is there to this day.

Despite his wound, Black Dog ran into the distance as if his life depended on it. The Captain stood staring after him in a bewildered state. He ran his hands over his eyes, and then suddenly he fainted. The Captain was laid out on the floor when my mother came running down the stairs. She called for me and we both managed to raise his head. He looked pale as death.

We could see his wound but could do nothing to help him until Dr. Livesey arrived and examined him. "He's had a stroke," he said matter-of-factly.

The doctor sent me for water and then ripped up the Captain's sleeve, which revealed many tattoos. There was one of a man hanging from a noose, beneath which read the name BILLY BONES.

"Well," said the doctor, "we must now try to save this Billy Bones' life." And with that, he opened the Captain's vein. Blood started pouring out, and then the Captain awoke, crying, "Where is Black Dog?"

"There is no Black Dog here. You've had a stroke and I've saved your life—and that against my will."

So saying, the doctor and I with much trouble helped the Captain into his bed. He had drawn enough blood for the Captain to lie at rest for a week. One more stroke like that, the doctor warned, and he would be finished for good.

CHAPTER 3

The Black Spot

⌒

When next I saw the Captain, he was pulling himself up from his bed and begging me to come closer. I did so, and then he barked out: "I can't lie here for a week. I've been seeing visions of Old Flint himself! Now, tell me," he said, "have you seen that sailor?"

I asked him if he meant Black Dog.

"No, not Black Dog, there's worse than him. They may hand me the death note we call a Black Spot, and they're after my sea chest. Now ride to get the doctor and tell him to call all hands to me here. I was Flint's first mate and I'm the only one knows where the treasure's at. He told me where it was hid before he died. Keep your eye open for the man with one leg and Black Dog and I'll share it all with you, upon my honor."

With that, he collapsed, but I did not ride to seek the doctor's help because that very night my kind father passed away. His death was so sudden, I could hardly spare a moment to think of the Captain. He would upset us all with his bad behavior on the very night before the funeral. As we mourned, he sang old sea songs, scowling and growling like an old blind dog.

And then, the day after the funeral, I was sitting out by the back door just thinking of my father, when a strange blind man drew near, hunched over a knobbly old stick. He called out, asking where he was, and I answered the Admiral

Benbow. When he drew close, I saw that he was eyeless and hooded and, suddenly, he had my wrist in a deathly grip.

"Now, boy," he said, "take me to the Captain or I will break your arm! Take me to him, and when we are near, say 'Here is a friend for you, Bill!'"

He then twisted my arm hard and marched me into the inn, where I yelled out as he had commanded. The Captain sat up, suddenly fully awake, looking terrified and mortally sick. He tried to rise but was too weak.

"Now, Bill, sit where you are," said the blind man, "I can't see, but I can feel a finger stirring. Business is business. Now, hold out your left hand. Boy, take his left hand by the wrist and bring it near to my right." I did as he told me and he dropped something from his hand into the Captain's.

"There," he said, "that's done." And without

uttering another word he leapt out the door with terrible speed. When the Captain regained his sense, he looked into his palm with horror, saying "Ten o'clock! Six hours left. We'll get them yet!"

With that, he sprang to his feet, suddenly clutched his throat, and fell to my feet. I ran to him, but all in vain. He had died and, though I never liked him, I burst into tears. It was the second death I had known in the space of two days.

CHAPTER 4

Blind Man's Bluff:
The Sea Chest Is Opened

⌐∽

I told my mother all that I knew, and both of us realized that the Captain's terrible shipmates would soon be coming for his chest and that we would never get the money we were owed. We heard footsteps in the dark and were haunted by visions in the mist.

We made up our minds to go to the nearest town to seek help, and were soon running scared. We ran on through the night and were happy to see the lights of the town burning brightly. But it was all for nothing. When we told the townspeople what had happened and mentioned the name Captain Flint, they all hid, afraid to help us. They would seek out the doctor's aid, but they would not help us defend our inn.

My mother cursed the men and told them we would risk returning alone. All they would do was to give me a loaded pistol and to promise to have horses for us when we returned in case we needed them. We headed back home in the dark moonless night through drifting fog. We somehow found our way back to the Admiral Benbow, where we bolted the door behind us, having only the Captain's dead body for company.

I reached down to his hand and found the crumpled paper he had so feared getting: the one with the words on it that read, *"You have till 10."* Suddenly, our clock began chiming and we heard that it was only six and were cheered: we still had four hours before anything could happen. I felt through his pockets for the key but found only a pocketknife and compass. My mother suggested that it might be around his neck, so I tore open his shirt and there, sure enough, hanging on a string, was the key.

We hurried to his room and spotted the old, battered chest. My mother quickly turned the key in the lock and had it open. Inside were carefully cleaned unworn clothing, pistols, silver, and trinkets from faraway lands. Beneath those things were parchment scrolls and a sack of gold. My mother insisted on taking only what was owed us. As we sat counting out the foreign coins, I grabbed her arm hard, holding a finger to my mouth.

From the street, I heard the tapping of the blind man's cane and then heard him pulling at the lock of the door. When it wouldn't open, we heard him retreat, tapping, into the night.

"Mother," I said, "let's take it all and go!" But

she would not. And then, suddenly, we heard a whistle from the street and she quickly changed her mind.

"I'll take what I have!" she exclaimed.

"And I'll take this bundle of old papers to make it even."

With that, we jumped up and sprinted downstairs, opened the door, and ran into the street. As we went on our way, the mist began to disappear and we saw that we were not a moment too soon. The moon rose high and we would have been exposed had we stayed still. Again, we heard voices coming our way, and my mother turned to me.

"Take this money, I'm going to faint." As she did

so, I caught her in my arms and dragged her under the low bridge by the Admiral Benbow. We could still hear the voices within earshot of the inn. I crouched as low as I could.

CHAPTER 5

The Last of the Blind Man

⟡

Curiosity drove out fear. I crept from under the bridge to the edge of the road and watched as my enemies' heads rose up out of the mist. They were led by the blind man, and soon seven or eight of them had reached the door.

"Down with the door!" he cried and soon, they were rushing at it, surprised to find it open. Their terrible leader urged them on. They were in the Admiral in a moment and suddenly, I heard a startled cry—"Bill's dead!"

The blind man told them to stop their

blubbering and to search his body for the key. They rushed up the stairs, threw open the window, and started yelling—"Listen, Old Pew! Someone's been here before us. The chest is torn apart but the money's here!"

"Drat the money!" he answered, "where is Flint's Fist? Is it on his body?"

The men searched but found him bare. Then Blind Man Pew cried out, "It's that boy—I wish I had put his eyes out. They were just here; they had the door bolted just before. They must be close. Fan out and find them!"

They roared through the inn, knocking things about as they tried to find us. Then we heard a whistle from the hill ring out two times.

"That means it's Dirk," said one man, "we'll have to get a move on now!"

But Pew lashed out at them, calling Dirk a coward and all of them fools for not searching harder.

"Find it and we'll live like kings! You were all too cowardly to face Bill, all except for me, and I was blind!" And with that, Pew began to strike at them with his cane, causing a great uproar among them.

Soon they were fighting like cats and dogs. Suddenly, the sound was broken by that of hooves and the ring of a pistol shot. The buccaneers turned and ran in every direction. Only Pew was left, tapping and cursing and crying out their names as he passed right by me. When he heard the riders, he spun and ran in a panic, slipping beneath one of their horses. He fell at their feet, now quite still.

I soon saw it was a boy from the town and several officers. They immediately understood what had happened and took off in pursuit, slowed down by the weather and the need for their horses to go up steep hills. When they arrived at the docks, they saw that a small boat had already been set loose and that the scoundrels had escaped scot-free. My mother had recovered in the inn, but not old blind Pew. The man was more dead than stone.

At the inn, we discovered everything in a wreck. After telling them my story, the head officer understood that it was the scroll in my jacket they were after. We quickly decided to make our way to Dr. Livesey's house to get it put away for safekeeping. With that, an officer helped me onto the back of his horse and I was off again, into the night.

CHAPTER 6

The Captain's Papers

W̲e rode hard to Dr. Livesey's with the head officer, Mr. Dance, leading the way. We got down from our horses but found the doctor out and went on to find him at dinner with the Squire. We were quickly let in and brought to the great library. Dr. Livesey was chatting with the Squire, surrounded by shelves of books.

The Squire was quick to ask what our business was, but once they knew, I could see their interest and desire to know more. They were cheered that we had returned to the inn, and Mr. Trelawney, the Squire, began to pace the floor.

"Mr. Dance," he said, "you are a noble fellow and shouldn't waste time worrying about trampling that blind mischief maker. The boy Hawkins here is as good as gold."

It was then decided that we should see what this packet contained. Two of the men had a servant fetch me something hot to eat, which I devoured. Mr. Dance and the doctor talked over various matters, but soon the conversation returned to recent events. The doctor asked if the Squire had heard of this man Flint.

"Heard of him! He is the most bloodthirsty pirate who ever sailed. All pirates feared him, and I once even saw his sails off Trinidad! The richest and meanest pirate of them all was Flint!"

They all thought that there must be some clue to a great treasure in the packet. If this was so, the Squire would provide a ship and use it to search out the treasure, no matter the cost. Dr. Livesey agreed and set it down on the table. We quickly cut open its stitching and found that it contained a book and a sealed paper. They agreed to try the book first and invited me to look closer and share in the discovery. Dr. Livesey and I were puzzled by its strange markings and figures in columns, but the Squire knew what we held in our hands.

"This is that black-hearted rascal's account book!" And so it was, a ledger of ships boarded, fortunes stolen, and moneys owing in French, Spanish, and English coin.

We then turned our attention to the sealed packet. When the doctor opened it, a map fell out with notes and directions, along with longitudes and latitudes. And just past a hill marked "The Spyglass," we saw a note that read *"bulk of treasure here."* There were further directions to a place called Skeleton Island.

The Squire was overjoyed and commanded that a great ship be found and a journey commenced at once.

"I shall be Admiral. You, Livesey, will be ship's doctor; and Hawkins here our cabin boy! And we'll bring along my own men—Redruth, Joyce, and Hunter."

He was thrilled, and his face showed it. But the doctor had one thing to say.

"The only man I am afraid of is you, Trelawney, for you cannot hold your tongue! There are pirates out there who will kill for this, and who will take any risks to get at it. We must stay together until our ship is at sea. I will stay with Jim, but none of us must speak a word about any of this."

And with that, the Squire promised to be silent as the grave.

CHAPTER 7

The Crew Is Assembled

⌒

It took time to get ready. The doctor and the
Squire both had work to do. I stayed at the hall
under the watch of Redruth, the gamekeeper,
waiting with eagerness. I spent my time studying
the map and imagined how our journey would
be: thick with danger and enemies and intrigue.
But, of course, nothing I imagined was as strange
and tragic as what occurred when our true journey began.

One day a letter came, addressed to Dr. Livesey or myself. I opened it with Redruth standing

next to me, and scanned its message. The Squire had found a ship called the *Hispaniola*, which he purchased from a man named Blandly. This man, by his own admission, had been in town, talking of the treasure we would soon be sailing for. He had stumbled upon an old sailor, down on his luck, who offered to be the ship's cook and who could help put together a crew.

"Long John Silver he is called, and has lost a leg in his country's service. He has no pension and I took him on immediately. He is a great man and we are lucky to have him!"

Furthermore, Long John Silver had helped him pick a crew for our journey, including a first mate named Arrow. The letter finished with the Squire's excitement about our voyage and recommended I should spend one night with my mother before leaving.

I found her in good health and was happy to see that the Squire had had the inn repaired and repainted. He had also sent her an apprentice, and when I saw that I had been replaced, I wept. I had only been thinking of my adventures, but now I understood that I was truly leaving home. The next morning, as we walked away from the inn, I thought of Captain Billy Bones and the way he had walked along the shore. The Admiral Benbow was soon out of sight.

We next went by coach to Bristol. I saw that the quay and the docks were a busy, furious place with the smell of tar and salt. There were sailors with rings in their ears, and some who wore pigtails, while others walked by like proud peacocks. I thought that now I was going to be one of them and was delighted! We then met the Squire, who was dressed like a ship's Admiral in all his finery.

"Oh sir," I cried, "when do we sail?"

"We sail tomorrow!" he answered.

CHAPTER 8

At the Sign of the Spyglass

∽

After breakfast, the Squire sent me to go meet John Silver at the sign of the Spyglass. I made my way there and found a neat tavern full of seafaring men who talked loudly, rarely stopping their singing and laughing. I saw a man with his leg cut off at the hip and knew it had to be Long John.

He carried a crutch and hopped with great speed, cheerful and laughing among the customers. Now, I had long worried that this might be the one-legged man whom the Captain was so afraid of, but seeing him, I knew he was a very

different sort from Pew, the Captain, and Black
Dog. So I approached him and handed him the
Squire's letter. He shook my hand firmly and
smiled.

"So you are our new cabin boy!" he said loudly.

Suddenly, a man jumped up from the bar and
made for the street. I knew at once by his look and
missing fingers who it was. I cried out that I had
just seen Black Dog.

"I don't care who he is, he shall pay for his vile
deeds!" said Long John, and sent one of his men
after him. He then quizzed me about the man and
said he had never heard the name. Then he
grabbed the man who had been talking to Black
Dog. He admitted that the blind beggar had also
been in the bar and told us that his name
was . . . Pew!

Long John became quite excited about track-
ing down Black Dog and assured me that his man
Ben would find him.

"Talking of throwing someone overboard, was he? It's him I'll throw overboard if I get the chance!"

As he ranted, Long John walked up and down with his one leg and his crutch, cursing Black Dog and all those like him. Seeing Black Dog had made me suspicious, but John Silver had put on a good show. I was sure he was an innocent man, and he was clever at convincing me. He told me how worried he was that I would think badly of him for having such low-life persons in his tavern. He made me believe that if only he'd had his other leg, he would have caught the man himself.

We decided to report to Mr. Trelawney right away and so began our journey down to the water. There he laughed, told old sea stories, and explained the different kinds of boats to me. He told me of their cargo and the way they were made and repeated phrases until I knew them like an old sailor. I began to think of him as the best of all shipmates.

When we arrived, Dr. Livesey was there. Long John told the story to both men in lively fashion and asked for my agreement regarding what had happened. I simply nodded yes to everything he said. When he had finished, he made his way back to the tavern, and we all agreed to be on board by four that afternoon.

"Well, Trelawney, I don't put much stock in your judgment," said the doctor, "but Silver is an ace! Now, Jim," he said to me, "let's go see our ship!"

CHAPTER 9

The Captain Has Doubts

＄

We swiftly made our way to the harbor, where the *Hispaniola* lay beside the other great ships. Then we met the mate, Mr. Arrow, whose earrings and squinty eye made us look twice. Shortly after, we met Captain Smollett, who asked to speak immediately to both the Squire and the doctor in the Squire's cabin.

"Well, Captain Smollett," said Mr. Trelawney, "what have you to say?"

The Captain scowled and refused to mince words. He was a plainspoken man.

"I don't like the men and I don't like my officer. That's short and sweet."

Of the ship he had no complaints, but he went
on to relate that he felt the men already knew too
much about our quest for treasure. And he didn't
think it right that he knew less than they did
about our journey.

"I don't like treasure voyages and I certainly
don't like secret journeys of which even the
cook's parrot has been informed. He's blabbed of
the treasure already. I think it's a dangerous voyage we are about to take."

He complained of many other things, and
asked if we were determined to go on with our
treasure journey.

"Like iron!" answered the Squire.

"Well then," replied the Captain, "I suggest we
separate the powder from the arms. I also suggest
that all of your own men sleep in the same area
beside the cabin. Finally, I suggest there be no

more mention of this treasure. The crew already knows the exact location of the island."

To this, the Squire protested that he had told no one, and we believed him. But somehow the crew had gotten wind of our journey and our goal—and that was a dangerous bit of news.

"I don't know," added the Captain, "who has the map, but I demand that it be kept even from Mr. Arrow or I shall resign."

It was clear that the Captain feared a mutiny, and only the doctor's assuring words were able to return him to a calm state. As for Mr. Trelawney, he took offense and scowled at the Captain.

"I have heard you and will do as you ask; but I do not think better of you for it."

This the Captain shrugged off, and we were soon out on deck examining our fine ship. I was shown my hammock and the arrangements of powder and weapons—and our sleeping berths were soon changed.

Long John Silver and two other men arrived on board shortly after and tried to protest our changes, but the Captain sent them sharply belowdecks.

"That's a good man, Captain," said the doctor.

But it was clear the Captain was reserving judgment on his entire crew—he even sent me with a sharp word belowdecks to help Long John, saying he would have no favorites on the ship. By then, I guarantee you, I disliked him intensely.

CHAPTER 10

What I Heard in the Apple Barrel, and Afterward

⌒

We worked well into the night. I was thrilled with the sea talk and quick banter of the men. As we worked, Long John raised up his crutch like a baton and started up his fast-paced sea chantey:

"Fifteen men on a dead man's chest—"
And the whole crew joined in with,
"Yo-ho-ho and a bottle of rum!"

Even then, in my excitement, it brought me back to our own Captain at the inn. Before I knew it, we were on our voyage to Treasure Island.

The voyage was long and the *Hispaniola* soon proved itself to be an able vessel that sped us along on our journey. Not so with Mr. Arrow. He often seemed seasick, and though the doctor tried to look after him, he stumbled about on deck and had to be helped into bed as often as not. One day, he disappeared entirely.

"Well," said Captain Smollett, "that's a relief. Overboard and good riddance." And with this, the Captain had to find a new mate, and did so in Israel Hands, the wily old seaman who was a great friend of Long John Silver.

Long John himself turned out to be a great seaman in his own way. He was quick and nimble and ever helpful, and the men loved him dearly. I spent much of my time by his side in the galley, helping with the cooking, with Long John and his parrot for my only company.

"I call my parrot," he told me, "Cap'n Flint, after the famous pirate!"

At this, the parrot would squawk out "Pieces of eight, pieces of eight!" and would carry on until his master covered the cage with a shred of torn sail. He then told me of its great age and the parrot's many voyages. During this time, we drew close, and I thought him the best of men and a true friend.

In the meantime, Captain Smollett and the Squire remained distant. Everything about the Captain's displeasure interfered with Mr. Trelawney's sense of adventure and joy at being aboard. The crew, on the other hand, never had an easier time of it, I imagine. There was good wind and good food for all, and even a big barrel of apples on deck at all times for any to take his pick of the sweet fruit.

All of this the Captain considered taking away

from us, but as you will see, the apple barrel did eventually serve its purpose. If not for that barrel, we might have had no warning and might all have been killed in a foul manner.

Late one day, as the sun was going down, I chose to go and find an apple for myself out of the barrel and, finding it nearly empty, crawled right in to get to the bottom. Once inside, I sat there with the darkness coming on and began to feel quite sleepy.

Suddenly, though, I heard a muffled voice and sensed a body leaning against the barrel that I knew to be Silver himself. After hearing only the first few words, I trembled with fear, for now I knew that the lives of the few honest men left on board depended on me alone. The fearful whispering continued.

"Flint was Captain and I was quartermaster. It was on that voyage," continued Silver, "that I lost my leg and Pew lost his eyes. That ship was

dripping with red blood and fit to sink with all the gold we found."

I soon heard that he was spinning yarns for the youngest hand on deck, who was thrilled with his tales. I blushed to hear him use the same compliments on this lad that he had used on me. I knew then that I had been played for a fool. I was filled with rage and shame.

"We gentlemen of fortune live rough and lean but when we get back to shore, we carry hundreds of pounds, not handfuls of coins. I began just like you but made my fortune at sea. By now, my wife has sold my tavern and taken all my money—we'll meet up again one day I'm sure. Oh, on our journeys, some feared Flint and some feared Pew, but all feared Long John Silver. That was the roughest crew afloat—the Devil himself would have been afraid to sail with them. I tell you I am not a boasting man, but you may be sure of yourself on old John's ship."

It was clear the lad was under his influence, and Silver continued to flatter and stroke him. Soon enough, as John continued to talk of gentlemen of fortune, I understood that he meant pirates, and that he himself was one. By and by, Israel, one of the crew, came up to talk with them.

"Look here, John and Dick," he said, "how long are we going to stand off? I've had enough of Captain Smollett, by thunder!"

Then Silver turned hard on the man. "You'll attack now and take away the Captain who can steer this ship to the treasure, all for a better berth to lay your scurvy head in! You'll wait and you'll act only on my signal!"

"And then," asked Israel, "what do we do with *them*?"

"My vote," said Long John, "is death. When

I'm living like a king later, I don't want survivors coming back to have me hanged. Now, Dick, have yourself a sweet apple from this here barrel, courtesy of me."

With this, I froze, for I knew the game was over. I thought of running, but could find no strength. But Israel himself saved my life, saying he was too excited by the thought of their mutiny to eat anything more that day. Long John laughed a wicked laugh, while Israel headed belowdecks.

Suddenly, the moon came up and the call went out over the sail as the lookout shouted, "Land ho!"

With that, all the ship's men were on deck, trying to stare through the fog at our destination. The Captain gave out orders and asked if any had seen this island. To my surprise, Long John's voice rang out, admitting he had once stayed there.

When the Captain asked him where we might anchor, John answered him clearly.

"Skeleton Island they call it. It was a pirates' place at one time, but no more. That hill is the Fore-Mast hill and that big one The Spyglass, as they used it for a lookout."

With that, the Captain produced a chart for Silver to see. As the pirate leaned forward I saw his disappointment, for this was a new chart that laid out the island, but with no red crosses or written notes leading to the treasure. Silver still pointed out where we might anchor and complimented the Captain on bringing us so speedily to our destination. I was now truly frightened of Silver, and as he drew up to me, I shivered.

"Oh, Hawkins son, this is a sweet spot, this island. I'll pack you a lunch and we'll go and spend an afternoon exploring. I remember being here as a youth myself."

With that, he clapped me on the shoulder and left me while I turned my attention to the doctor. I hurriedly told him that something terrible had happened and that he should find an excuse to get belowdecks with the Captain and Mr. Trelawney and then to call me down, too. He wasted no time explaining the situation to the Captain, who called all hands to deck.

"Lads," he said, "this is the island we've been sailing for. And, to celebrate, Mr. Trelawney will provide double rations today and tomorrow for every sailor aboard. Please excuse us now while we go belowdecks and have a feast for ourselves!"

With that, there was a cheer for the Squire and the Captain, led by Long John himself, that treacherous pirate. Then the three men headed belowdecks and soon called me to join them.

"Well, Hawkins," said the Squire, "speak your mind."

With that, I told them all that had happened.

They then sat me down, patting me on the back and congratulating me for all the good work I had done.

"I have been a fool," the Squire said. But the Captain was quick to confess that he, too, had been taken in by the crew's hard work. Now they all cursed Long John Silver's name for leading them astray. It was time to figure out how many honest men were still on board. We counted no more than seven.

"There's nothing to do but wait until we know who is honest and who is not. We shall have to lay back and wait and see—that's the best we can do."

"Hawkins," said the Squire, "I put my faith in you—whatever you can find out will be important to us."

With this I felt deep fear. There were six of us (seven, if I included myself), against nineteen hardened pirates.

CHAPTER 11

How My Shore Adventure Began

The next morning, the island looked quite different. Its gray solemn forests and stretches of golden sand, its three distinct hills topped by the Spyglass itself, all put fear in my heart. The ship rocked and I felt seasick and ill and thought my adventure ruined, for I now hated the very thought of Treasure Island.

Throughout the heat of the day, we worked away quietly. But the crew had suddenly become surly and mean. Only Long John tried to keep them from seeming so. It became obvious that mutiny was upon us, and as we drew up to the cove where we would moor, not a sound stirred—the only thing we could hear was the crashing of the waves. We who had met in council only the night before knew that Long John's worry was the worst proof we could have. We met once again in the cabin to try to decide upon the course that was best.

"If I give another order," said the Captain, "there will be mutiny. And if I don't, Silver will know that I am laying back because I know of his plan. Then we'd be done for."

"Well," said the Squire, "what can we do?"

"I propose," said the Captain, "sending the men ashore for an afternoon. If all go over to Silver's side, we must fight the ship. If none do, we hold the cabin only. But if only some go, mark my words, Silver will bring them back calm and in order. As mild as lambs."

And so it was decided. We brought Hunter,

Joyce, and Redruth into our plan and gave each a pistol. The Captain went to the deck and announced the free leave.

"As many as would like," he offered, "may go ashore. I will fire a gun a half hour before sundown to let you know when to return to the ship."

With that, the men jumped up as if they thought they would find treasure the minute they stepped from the boat. They ceased looking downcast and were bright and chipper. The Captain quickly went below and, sure enough, Silver organized the men as if he were already their Captain.

The honest men who went along were just dullards, or were lazy and idle. Most had let themselves be led astray in order to avoid having to work. But it is altogether another thing to join in a plot to take a ship and murder innocent men. At the end, thirteen men went ashore and six stayed on board.

It was then that I became either brave or stupid, I can't say which, but I decided to hide myself in one of the boats. It was not the boat Silver was in but he saw that I had slipped aboard, and called out my name more than once.

When our boat landed at the beach first, I leapt out and, taking off into the trees, disappeared into the forest. I had begun to regret my decision, but I ran and kept running until I could run no more.

CHAPTER 12

The Man of the Island

∽

I was thrilled to have given Silver the slip and began to enjoy exploring the island. It was full of strange things to see—enough to excite the imagination and curiosity of any boy my age. I wish I could remember all of them, but my young mind was overwhelmed at the time with all the vivid new colors and sights. I could have spent a month just taking in all the strange plants and trees I came upon. I had marched across some marshy tract of land full of swaying willows and bulrushes (which I had read about in the Bible) and

odd-shaped trees that rose up out of the swamp.
Then there was some wave-like, sandy country
that went on for about a mile. There you could see
pines and twisted-looking trees that resembled
oak, except for their purplish tinge. In the distance
I could see one of the hills with its craggy peak
shining brightly beneath the harsh sun.

Now I really began to feel like I was an
explorer—I felt free and full of joy, forgetting for a
time the many dangers I was facing. The island was
truly uninhabited. My shipmates were left behind,
and before me nothing lived but unfamiliar birds
and other creatures that went running or flying
for cover as soon as I approached. There were tor-
toises with backs so large they looked like bathing
tubs, and magical flowering plants of a size and
shape you only come upon in dreams.

Suddenly I heard a rustle among the bulrushes—a wild duck flew up with a quack, then
another followed, and then another. Soon, along

the whole surface of the marsh, a great cloud of birds hung screaming and circling in the air. I knew my shipmates must be coming up close, so I ran quickly and crouched behind the nearest tree not far from the swamp, and waited, silent as a mouse. I heard voices and among them one I knew to be Silver's. I overcame my fear and crawled closer to catch the meaning of their words.

"You're more valuable than gold to me. That's why I'm warning you now. You can't change the plan, you can only save yourself by joining in. Come on now, Tom, tell me what they would do to me if they knew I was telling you all this now?"

"Silver," said Tom, "you may have let yourself be led away, but not me. I'd sooner lose my hand than turn against . . ."

Suddenly, we all heard a cry of anger and then, a terrible, drawn-out scream. The noise echoed across the crags of the Spyglass and the birds rose again in a rush. I knew it was a death cry, and Tom jumped to his feet.

"What was that?" he asked.

"That," answered Silver, "that'll be Alan."

"Alan!" cried out Tom, "well then, rest his soul. And as for you, Long John Silver, you're no mate of mine. I may die, but if I do, it will be for duty's sake. You've killed Alan, have you? Well, I defy you to kill me!"

And with that, Tom started running away. But Silver, full of new strength, steadied himself, leaned back, and aimed his crutch. Its point drove at the center of Tom's back and he fell with a cry. I had no time to tell if this had hurt him badly. Silver was soon on him and, with his knife out, had driven two quick stabs into him to end his life.

I heard Silver panting. I felt faint, but managed not to pass out as I watched him wipe the blood from his knife. The whole scene was playing over in my mind. Silver then pulled a whistle from his pocket and blew it twice. I knew that the other men would be coming quickly now and, if they had killed those two honest men, would they not kill me? I began to crawl back and, as I did so, I heard a chorus of voices ring out.

I turned, racing through the thicket until I ran only on fear. I needed to return to the ship with the men, but how could I? As I thought it through again, I knew they would wring my neck if I tried. I said my silent good-byes to the *Hispaniola*, to the doctor, and to the Squire and Captain. I knew there remained for me only death by starvation or at the hands of the mutineers.

Yet I continued to make speed through the trees, until I was at the foot of a little hill. There, my heart thumping, a fresh alarm brought me to a standstill.

Suddenly, I saw a shadow move just beyond my eye and knew I was not alone. I stood stock still as I saw it run past me, almost doubled over. I could not tell if it was man or monkey. I started running again and saw that it was set on cutting me off and so became more afraid of it than of Silver. But I readily remembered that I had a pistol with me and turned briskly to face this mountain man. He stepped out of the trees and walked toward me.

"Who are you?" I asked.

"Ben Gunn," he answered with a voice rusty and awkward from lack of use. "I'm poor Ben Gunn and I haven't spoken to a soul in three years!"

I could see now he was a man like me, however sunburned and bearded he was. His lips were cracked, and he was dressed in rags made from pieces of old ships' canvas. I asked if he had been shipwrecked.

"No, marooned!" he answered.

I had heard this word before and knew what it meant: a terrible punishment, where someone accused of a crime is left all alone on an island to fend for himself. Then he told me how he had survived on goats, berries, and oysters, and that he had long dreamed of eating cheese once again.

"Well," I told him, "if I can get back on my ship, you shall have it!"

I then told Ben my name and he told me with a crazed grin and in a whisper a great secret.

"Jim," he hissed, "I have nothing, but I am rich!"

He went on to tell me that he would make me a rich man, too, and asked quickly if my ship was Flint's. Suddenly, I trusted him, and told him that the ship was not Flint's and that Flint was dead.

And that some of the men were Flint's and were mutineers and murderers.

"Not a man—with one—leg?" he gasped.

"Yes, Silver is their leader," I answered, seeing him shiver.

I told him at that point all that had happened.

"Do you think," he asked, "if I could help, that the Squire would take me on and perhaps let me keep one thousand pounds of this money?"

I answered that he would of course do so. Then Ben revealed to me that he had been on board with Flint's men when Flint had gone ashore with six men and buried the treasure. These six he had somehow killed with his own hands and had never told a soul on board where the treasure was. Those who asked were told they were welcome to stay on the island and try to find the treasure. Of course, they all said no.

But poor Ben was back with another ship three years later and, upon seeing the island, had told the crew he could find the treasure. After three days of searching, they cursed his name and left him to fend for himself, leaving him only a musket, a spade, and a shovel.

"But you tell your Squire," he said, "that when not pining for home and for cheese, Ben has been occupied with another matter that should interest him."

I answered that of course I would but that I had no way of getting back to the ship.

"Well," said Ben, pointing to a cove, "we could always in a pinch use this little boat that I have made. I keep it by a white rock that lies farther down toward the shore."

And with that, we heard cannon fire and gunshots ringing out through the air. The sun was still high in the sky. I knew that the fighting aboard ship had begun. Ben kept me low and out of sight. Then he pointed some distance ahead to where the English flag fluttered in the wind.

CHAPTER 13

The Story Continued by the Doctor: How the Ship Was Abandoned

That afternoon when the two boats went ashore, the Captain, the Squire, and I sat talking matters over while keeping an eye on the six mutineers left on board who were sitting and skulking. Hunter came down to tell us that Jim had gone ashore and our hearts sank.

We came to a decision, worried for his safety, and saw immediately that Hunter and I should go ashore and find out more. We headed directly for the stockade that had appeared on the map and found it to be a sturdy, well-protected place with a freshwater spring and a high fence. We thought it perfect for defense. With that, we heard the cry of a man dying and thought at once that it was Jim Hawkins, killed this time for sure.

We instantly rowed back to the *Hispaniola* and found the Squire white as a sheet and one of the six hands on deck looking equally pale. The Captain told me he thought that one might come over to our side. We quickly put Redruth in the galley between the cabin and the forecastle, with loaded muskets. Hunter brought the boat around and Joyce and I quickly loaded it with powder, guns, biscuits, kegs of pork, and my medicine chest. On deck, the Captain held the crew within range of his pistol, saying——

"Mr. Hands, there are two of us here who will shoot the first man that moves."

The crew was shocked but quickly went belowdecks, only to find Redruth waiting with his weapons. They came up again, but cowered under the Captain's guns. By this time we had the boat loaded and made quickly for shore.

We reached the stockade and, leaving Joyce as guard, quickly loaded in our wares without stopping. We then rowed back, exhausted, to the *Hispaniola*. Once more we loaded the boats with another round of cargo and got ready to set out for shore yet again.

First, though, we took all the guns we could and dumped the rest overboard, watching them all sink to the clean, sandy bottom. We heard voices calling out from shore and knew that our time was up. Before loading everything into the boat, the Captain called down to the men below-decks.

"I am speaking to you, Abraham Gray. I am leaving. I order you to follow your Captain. I don't think you are like those other men. I give you thirty seconds to join me. Come at once. I am risking my life for you and the lives of my friends here."

As soon as he finished, we heard a scuffle and Gray appeared with a knife cut on his face and ran to the Captain. With that, we jumped into our boat and headed out. We were clear of the ship but not yet on shore.

⁓

Now, as we came up to the shore, we found that our trip out this time was much slower. We were five men now and much too loaded down with cargo. Added to this was the fact that the tide was against us—the boat could be swamped and all of us drowned. Suddenly, the Captain spoke.

"The cannon!'" he exclaimed.

It was only then that we recalled the onboard cannon and its ammunition clearly laid out on deck. We turned to see the five pirates on board readying the gun to be shot our way, and our hearts went cold.

"Israel," said Gray, "was Flint's gunner." We knew then that an expert shot was taking aim at us.

All present nominated the Squire as the best shot. He at once stood up and aimed his rifle at the *Hispaniola* and, as he shot, we saw Israel duck and the man behind him fall. At the same time, we heard voices from the shore and saw men coming from the trees, pointing. Some were getting into the two boats, and others were running in one direction as we headed for a point from which we could make our escape.

We made our target and were sheltered from the men who were after us. Our main worry now was the cannon, which they were quickly reloading. They paid no attention to the fallen man and, just as the Squire reloaded, had the great gun ready.

As he pulled the trigger, they let loose their shot also, and this was the great blast heard by Jim.

We heard the terrible pellet go past us, close overhead. The boat shook from all this violence, and then the front portion of the boat went underwater.

Sure enough, the Squire and I managed to keep our guns above water, standing there in the shallow surf, but the rest of the men dropped into the water with the rest of our supplies. Their guns were ruined, and we now found we had only two left and that all our provisions were gone. To add to our troubles, we heard voices coming near and, in such a crippled state, feared being cut off from our home stockade.

We waded ashore as fast as we could, the poor jolly-boat sinking and, along with it, half of our gunpowder and supplies.

CHAPTER 14

The Doctor Continues:
The First Day of Fighting Ends

⌒○

We now ran to the stockade and at every step heard the pirates drawing closer. As we made for the clearing, the Captain passed his best gun to the Squire, who raised it to his shoulder and took aim. I turned and gave my sword to Gray, who, I am happy to say, spit on his hands and, taking it, made it sing as he slashed the blade through the sharp air. He had come back to the right side.

We were advancing to our stockade when some of the mutineers appeared. They stopped suddenly and the Squire and I fired, just as Hunter and Joyce did from the stockade. One of the enemy fell dead, shot through the heart. The rest scattered.

Just as we were beginning to feel victorious, a shot rang out and poor Tom Redruth fell to the ground. It was plain he was dying. The rest of the mutineers had retreated, so we carried poor Tom back to our stockade, and there, after requesting prayers and asking forgiveness from the Squire, he died.

The Captain then emptied his pocket of the many small items he had been carrying, such as pen, rope, ink, tobacco and a logbook. He climbed to the roof of the log house and there tied the flag of England to the top of a fallen tree he had with many pains drawn up. Finishing this, he came back down and asked me how many weeks before I expected another ship would come to find us if we had not returned. I answered that it would more likely be months, not weeks, before that happened. The Captain then answered that we were very tight on rations.

"It's a shame we lost that second load. We're much in trouble without it."

Just then, we heard the cannon fire again and heard a ball land just beyond the cabin. We knew then that they were firing for us, but we felt no alarm.

"Oho!" said the Captain, "blaze away. You'll never hit us from where you are, but you'll do us the favor of using up all your powder."

With that, the gun flared again, but to no purpose. They continued this all through the evening. Later that night, Gray and Hunter volunteered to try to rescue the rations from the shallow water where the low tide had left them in the sand. This proved useless, as Silver's men, they found, were already carrying most of them away. They had their arms around our supplies and each bore a musket, taken no doubt from some secret hiding place of their own.

The Captain began to record our condition in his log. "Alexander Smollett, master, David Livesey, ship's doctor, Abraham Gray, carpenter's mate, John Trelawney, owner, John Hunter and Richard Joyce, owner's servants, landsmen, being all that's left, with stores for ten days. Thomas Redruth, shot dead, James Hawkins . . ."

And, even as he was finishing, we heard a joyous shout—I ran out just in time to see Jim Hawkins safe and sound, climbing over the stockade wall.

CHAPTER 15

Jim Resumes the Story:
The Garrison in the Stockade

∽

As soon as Ben saw the flag flying, he sat me down and told me it was there I would find my friends. I thought it more likely the pirates would be there, but he told me that pirates would fly, not the British flag, but their dreaded Jolly Roger—the famous black flag with its skull and crossbones inscribed in white.

"That place was built by Flint himself, who was afraid of no man but Long John Silver!"

"Well," I answered, "let's go there before Silver himself finds us!"

But Ben, trusting no man, would not go. He made me swear that tomorrow I would send someone from our camp to meet him, as he had a proposal for us. He insisted one of us should come, holding up a white handkerchief for caution's sake.

"And if you run into Silver," he added, "don't let it be known that Ben Gunn is on this island. It would be the ruin of us!"

I promised I wouldn't and just then, a cannonball fell with a crash right by our side, setting each of us off and running in his own direction. The shots continued and I was sure they were chasing me. Soon enough, I came to a clearing and saw that the *Hispaniola* was offshore and flying the Jolly Roger.

I also saw what the pirates on shore were

up to. They were hacking the jolly-boat apart and throwing the wood into a blazing fire. These men, who had once been so gloomy as they rowed the light boats back and forth to the ship, were clapping and singing and being foolish and mean. I almost felt pity for men who could act so much like beasts.

I thought now was the time to make for the stockade and, while on the way, found the white rock where Ben had been hiding his boat. This information I stored in my mind in case I might need it later. I kept going and made my way over the fence to the stockade and into the party of my friends.

I soon told them my story and took stock of the log house. It would do, but it was smoky from our fire, not to mention poor Gray lying wrapped in a bandage on account of his knife cut, and poor Tom cold and dead under a flag in the corner of the room.

The Captain, however, wisely kept us all busy with chores, collecting firewood and digging a grave for Redruth. I spoke to the doctor about Ben, and he told me he had something special for him.

"In my handkerchief," he said, "I have a piece of Parmesan cheese from Italy that we shall give him."

A meeting was held and we found when we counted only fifteen mutineers left. Two were wounded and one, who'd been shot by the cannon, probably was dead. We knew that the climate and the mosquitoes would soon affect the remaining men and that they might soon be sick and in a bad way.

"They might simply decide to get back in the ship, head out to sea, and return to being pirates," said the doctor.

The Captain grumbled, but he knew that losing his first ship might prove best for all of us in the long run.

Suddenly, we heard a voice rise up.

"There's a flag of truce! It's Long John Silver himself!"

With that, I rubbed my eyes and ran to peer through a loophole in the wall.

$$\backsim$$

We could see two men, one of them being Silver, indeed waving the white flag.

"Who goes there?" said the Captain.

"Flag of truce," answered Silver. "Cap'n Silver to come aboard and make terms."

The Captain snorted at Silver calling himself Captain, and yet he promised not to harm Silver if he came to the stockade unarmed. He then hopped his way over the fence and made his way, painfully and slowly, up the hill and toward us. We could see that he was in his finest blue coat, with a frilled hat tipped far back on his head.

Once inside, the Captain refused to let him in the fort, and Silver was forced to sit in the sand across from the Captain.

"It's a mighty cold morning, sir, to be sitting in the sand outside."

The Captain shrugged this off, telling Silver that he had brought it upon himself.

"You're either the ship's cook or you're Captain Silver, in which case you're a mutineer and a pirate and you can hang!"

Silver saw how we were each guarding a point of the fort and greeted us all. He then suggested that the Captain had killed one of his men in the night while they were all making merry. I knew, with joy, that this had been the work of my new friend Ben Gunn.

"Well," said Silver, "here it is. We want the treasure. You want your lives. You have a chart and we want it. Now, I mean you no harm . . ."

With that, the Captain burst out in anger and

told Silver that he knew his entire plan and would have none of it.

Each stared into the other's eyes without speaking. It was like being at the theater watching a play.

"Now," said Silver after a moment, "you give us the chart and you have a choice. We'll take you back with us and drop you somewhere safe. Or you can stay here and we'll give you half of our stores. Now, that's fair dealing from me."

"Is that all?" asked the Captain. "If so, you hear me. Here is my offer. If you come up one by one, unarmed, I shall put the cuffs on each of you and take you home to a fair trial. If not, I'll see you all in Davy Jones' locker, drowned dead at the bottom of the sea. You can't find the treasure. You can't sail the ship. These are the last good words you'll have from me. Next, you'll have a bullet in the back. Now get out."

"Well, let's at least shake hands on it then," cried Silver.

"Not I," said the Captain, and we each refused in turn.

With that, Silver crawled his way across the land and when he finally got up, he spat in our freshwater spring.

"That's what I think of ye!" he said. "Laugh all you like. In an hour, you'll laugh out the other end. Those who die will be lucky!" And with that and a curse, he made his way to the fence, where his man dragged him over the side.

CHAPTER 16

The Attack

As soon as Silver disappeared, the Captain turned on us and gave us all his fury for having left our posts. All of us were ashamed except for Gray, who had stayed fast. We then loaded our guns and got ready for what was to come.

"I don't have to tell you what's coming," said the Captain. "We're outnumbered but we can fight if we hold to our discipline."

Each refreshed himself with a cup of cool water from our spring and got ready. We doused the fire but the smoke still lingered in the air. We each took our positions and then Joyce, the servant, asked if he was to shoot if he saw a man.

"Of course!" shouted the Captain. He then sat fuming and waiting. Without wasting time, Joyce shot into the woods, and his shot was returned by three smoking rounds of fire.

"Did you hit him?" asked the Captain.

"No sir," answered Joyce, "I believe not, sir."

From that moment, we knew the attack was on. Suddenly, a cloud of pirates began to run out of the woods straight for our fence. They swarmed over it like monkeys and we all fired. Three men fell but one nimbly jumped up and disappeared. Four others had made the fence and seven or eight continued to fire toward us with little effect, their shots falling short.

Soon, however, the four pirates fell on us fiercely, and our whole position was reversed. We had gone from having secure cover to being openly exposed. There were shots everywhere and groans and curses and the Captain called for us to draw our swords and fight hand-to-hand in the smoke.

I grabbed my sword and cut my knuckles and saw a pirate grab Hunter's gun and smash him with it. I saw the doctor slash a mutineer across the face and I heard the Captain yelling in an injured voice.

I turned to find Anderson, the pirate, scrambling above me, his sword high above his head. I had no time to be afraid, for I lost my footing and fell, head over heels, right down the hill. When I landed, I saw that one of the pirates was coming over the fence with his dagger in his mouth. And then, suddenly, the fight was over.

Gray had cut down one, and another had been shot just as he entered the house. A third, the doctor had cut down. The fourth was now turning tail and climbing over the fence.

The doctor cried for us all to fire, but we were

finished for now. Suddenly, as they fled, they were all gone, and I saw the cost we had paid. Hunter was laid out, stunned. Joyce was dead, shot through the head, and the Squire was holding the pale Captain.

"The Captain is wounded!" said Mr. Trelawney.

"How many did we take down?" asked the Captain.

"Five," answered the doctor.

The Captain was grimly satisfied with this.

"Well, now our chances look better, with our odds at four to nine. We were seven to nineteen before."

CHAPTER 17

How My Sea Adventure Began

The mutineers did not come back that day. They had had their fill of fighting. As for us, Hunter never did recover and died that night of his injuries. Captain Smollett was wounded badly but not permanently, the shot having gone through his shoulder and nicked his lung. He would survive, but was under the doctor's orders not to move.

Just after noon, the coast being clear, the doctor strapped on his pistols and headed silently out to his meeting with Ben. Gray thought him insane to do so under such conditions.

In the meantime, I sat thinking it unfair that I should just sit and wait. I soon snuck out, filled my pockets with biscuits, and decided on my own mission. I would go to find, for certain, if Ben's boat existed and was in good shape. I armed myself with pistols and powder and slipped out. It was foolish to do so, but I was only a boy. As it turned out, it helped save us all.

I headed quickly along the shore to the white rock and soon saw the ship rocking in the waves at the same place, the Jolly Roger still flying. I also saw Silver and the pirate, last seen coming over the fence, pulling back to shore from the boat. And I heard the squawking laughter of his parrot in the wind. Soon they were coming my way, and I hurried on toward the white rock.

Below it was the boat, well hidden. It was the simplest, lightest, most basic craft possible. It looked as if it were made by men hundreds of years ago. But it was light and it would float.

I soon had another notion that I could not get rid of. I thought I would take the boat out under cover of night to the *Hispaniola*. Then I would cut the ship loose and let it go ashore in the night in some other cove. I thought this would stop our pirates from taking to the seas to kill again. And, I thought, as careless and sloppy as they were, it should be easy to do.

I waited until the dark and fog had set in and ate my biscuit. Then I carried my little boat to the water. In the dark, I saw that there were only two lights. One was the fire of the defeated pirates spread out on the shore. The other was the *Hispaniola*. I waded out, set my boat in the water, and made for the ship.

∽

My new boat and I soon made it out into the surf and quickly found our way up close to the

Hispaniola. It took some time to get used to, but it was a fairly solid boat and light in the water. Soon enough, I had laid hold of the rope that anchored the ship, called the hawser. It was tight and taut and I knew that with one cut, the entire *Hispaniola* would go humming along in the tide.

I knew also that the taut hawser could snap and would kill me with its force if I let it. So I began to cut it slowly, fiber by fiber. Suddenly, as I finished cutting the final threads, it slipped under the water.

I had been hearing loud voices from the cabin and now realized that there was a fight on board and the angry voices were getting louder. I knew it was Israel Hands and another, the pirate with the blade in his teeth who had tried to scale the fence. I heard them call each other terrible names and then it got quiet for a moment. I could also hear the voices of the mutineers on shore and could hear songs being croaked out in raspy voices.

At last, a breeze came up and the ship moved sideways and began to draw away and I was suddenly caught up in the wake of the big boat. I thought I might be smashed, but somehow I was not. I now decided to pull myself up for a look into the cabin and saw the two men wrestling madly. They each had the other by the throat. I ducked down quickly and shut my eyes tight.

I heard more singing coming from the shore—

"Fifteen men on a dead man's chest—
Yo-ho-ho and a bottle of rum!
Drink and the Devil had done for the rest—
Yo-ho-ho, and a bottle of rum!"

Suddenly, I felt that the boat had increased in speed and opened my eyes to see that we had sped across the shore. The campfire was right behind me. We had been set on a new course and were

heading out to sea. I could see the ship was moving on a sideways course, and the sailors inside knew they were in real danger and had stopped fighting. They could tell disaster was afoot.

I stayed flat against the bottom of my little boat, eyes closed and shivering with fear. I expected an ocean death at any moment, imagining myself swept under by the immense waves. Soon, I grew numb and tired and slept, dreaming of home and the Admiral Benbow, far away from my terrors on the sea.

CHAPTER 18

My Cruise in a Coracle

⌒∽

My little boat, or coracle, was tossing toward the south end of Treasure Island when I awoke. I was racked by thirst and found myself in and out of giant waves that tossed me to and fro without stopping.

I could not paddle and I saw that I would be drowned or dashed to death on sharp rocks if I came closer to shore. And I saw what looked like giant slugs on the rocks. These, I later learned, were sea lions, barking in the sun.

I saw that I would never make shore and that I

was heading north toward the Cape of the Woods. I thought I might be able to land there. I was still rolling in the waves when I found a smooth swell. I noticed that if I just let the boat go on its own, I made progress. It moved on top of the waves like a leaf and I thought I might reach land.

But it was not to be. As I rolled up and down in the terrible sun, my brain burning and my throat dry, I drifted past the point of landing. What was I to do?

As I rounded the next cape, I saw an incredible sight. The *Hispaniola*, under full sail, was moving my way. At first, I thought it was going the other way. Then I thought the sailors had come out of their heavy sleep and were chasing me. When it made yet another strange move, I was confused, not knowing what to think.

Suddenly, I understood, as the great ship swayed back and forth, that no one was steering it. The men were either hiding themselves below-decks or had abandoned ship. And then, the idea occurred to me to try to take the ship and give it back to its Captain.

Could it be that I could get aboard and steer it back? If the frightened pirates were on board, could I tie them up and take the wheel? I was made brave by the idea and tried to make my way toward the ship. Tossing in the wind, it continued to sail toward me.

As I drew alongside, I saw that I had one chance. I could see the ship's shiny brass fixtures now and thought it might be easy. But the wind died and the ship stayed put. Then, just as suddenly, it began to spin toward me with the cabin window still open. It came around and I saw that it would spin by and the bowsprit, a wooden beam that jutted out in front of the ship, would be over my head. I jumped like a rocket from the boat into the air, catching the beam. Just as suddenly, the boat rose up and came down on my little craft, crushing it. I knew then that I had no way back home but upon the *Hispaniola*.

CHAPTER 19

I Strike the Jolly Roger and Let Israel Hands Lend a Hand

Swinging about on the bowsprit, I knew I would be tossed into the sea. With heart racing, I made my way crawlingly back onto the deck. My eyes took in a sight of disaster and despair. Mud was caked everywhere and a broken bottle rolled about, to and fro. I saw that the sails were all up but that the two watchmen lay in a heap on the deck.

I saw Israel and the other sailor roll with the wind, and though Israel moved, the other was stock still on his back, his face painted over with a horrible smile. He was dead in a pool of blood. Suddenly, Israel began to moan and roll around. I saw that he was wounded and sick and bleeding. I walked slowly toward his body and stood over it.

"Come aboard, Mr. Hands," I said ironically.

With this, he rolled over and called for something to drink—he was parched with thirst. I knew then that he would rouse himself. I had no time to lose. I ran belowdecks to find everything a disaster. There was mud and broken glass everywhere. Books were torn open and stores were scattered randomly. In the dim light, I searched for food and a keg of water. I found biscuits, pickled fruit, raisins, and some cheese. I brought these on deck and, after eating and drinking my fill, gave Hands some of the cheese and biscuit, as well as some of the water to drink.

"Are you much hurt?" I asked him.

He nodded and groaned and said, "Well, he's dead. Now, where did you come from?"

"I've come to take back the ship, and you'll call me Captain until further notice."

He looked at me sourly, but said nothing. I told him I would drop the Jolly Roger. I scampered up and cut the flag loose happily.

"There's an end to Long John Silver," I said.

"Well now," said Hands, "this man and me were going to sail the ship back. But now he's dead and we need two to sail it. So I propose you get me a kerchief to tie my bleeding leg with and I'll help you sail it back."

"I'm not stupid," I said. "I'm not going to sail back to Kidd's cove where Silver is."

"Well, I don't have much choice, do I? It's your ship now and I'm wounded, so I'll sail wherever you want, by thunder!"

And with that, we made a deal. I tied his wound and he ate a little and we both began to sail the ship back to shore. Soon we were on our way, but as he gained strength, I saw his wounded look turn to a sneer. He began to watch me closely and craftily as he eyed me at my work.

Now, under Israel's guidance, we made our way over the foamy deeps in the *Hispaniola*. We soon stopped again for another meal and began to talk.

"Well now, Captain," he said, " I wonder if you could go down belowdecks and get me my glass. These old eyes could use a little help setting our course."

He turned his gaze away from me and back out to sea. It was plain he was up to something and wanted me off deck. But I thought I could outsmart him.

"Of course," I said, "it won't take but a moment."

With that, I ran belowdecks and, taking off my shoes, came up just behind him by way of another passage. There, I could see him without being seen. I watched him come to life and drag himself with some effort toward the dead man. Once there, he pulled out a knife and, wiping the blood off, tucked it into his sleeve and scrambled back to his spot. It was clear he meant to have my life.

As I ran back below to find his spyglass, I realized that he needed me to steer us back to shore. Once there, I would be in trouble, but for the moment, I was safe.

I clambered back up on deck and handed him his sleek brass instrument.

"Now," he said, "you take my orders, Captain Hawkins, and we'll make shore in no time at all."

He showed me where we might come in, and I ran about setting sails and making sure that we hit our mark.

"Steady, steady, steady!" said Hands and, at the last moment, I turned us hard and we made for our shore. I was so caught up in the work that it wasn't until the last moment that I sensed him behind me. I wheeled about and cried out as I saw him lunge for me. I let go of the sail and it quickly snapped at him and stopped him dead. Before he could recover, I ran away, but he was determined to get me.

I quickly reached for my guns and pulled the trigger, only to find the seawater had made them useless. I cursed my stupidity and ran again. He moved swiftly for a wounded man and soon boxed me in on deck. I dodged one way and he feigned the other. We played at this for a bit, each wary of the other.

Then, suddenly, the ship struck the beach and the jolt threw us both into the air. When it stopped, the ship was tilted and there was no place to stand on deck. Hands was tied up with the dead man while I scrambled up to the top of the mast. There, I quickly primed my guns and made them ready. He looked up at me and sneered

evilly. He put his knife in his teeth and began a slow and painful climb up the mast after me. Soon enough, he was too close for my liking.

"One more step, Mr. Hands," I said, "and I'll blow your brains out." I even laughed a little, thinking myself the victor. He stopped. I could see his mind working slowly. He took the dagger from his mouth to speak.

"Well," he said, "we're caught. I would have had you if not for that landing. But I don't have no luck, not I."

I was smiling away when I noticed that his hand had slowly drawn back. He had reached his knife and let loose right at me, pinning my shoulder to the mast. I cried out in pain and, firing both pistols in shock, dropped them into the ocean. But they didn't fall alone. Israel Hands fell to a watery death along with them.

CHAPTER 20

Pieces of Eight

⌒

Hands sank into the water and I watched as a bubble of blood came up to the surface. I soon began to feel sick. I could not pry myself loose of the dagger and was terrified of falling from my spot to die alongside Israel. I then shuddered and by doing so tore the blade loose and was free. It turned out I was only pinned by the tiniest piece of my shoulder and mostly by my shirt.

I crawled down the mast and then, looking around, decided to throw the other dead man into the sea. This I did in a hurry. I tried to set the ship as right as I could so that it would not be hurt and then decided to take my leave.

I leapt off the deck of the *Hispaniola* and, in a happy frame of mind, headed for the forest. I thought about the hero's welcome I could expect and about the way I would be treated upon my return. I had been a fool, but my prize was the return of our ship, and I thought myself brave and lucky.

I walked on and then, as dusk fell, I walked closer and closer to where I had first met poor Ben, our island man. As the night got darker, I grew ever less sure of myself and kept tripping and rolling in sandy pits.

Soon enough, I found myself walking in moonlight—this helped but I still walked warily. I did not want to end my adventure by having my own party shoot me. Finally, as I came to the stockade, I saw the giant, smoldering remains of a fire. I wondered why there had been such a big fire. It went against the Captain's orders, to be sure.

I saw the blockhouse in shadow and not a soul stirring. I thought perhaps something had gone wrong while I had been away, so I began to creep on my hands and knees. As I got closer there was little doubt they had kept a bad watch. I got to the door and stood up. I could see nothing with my eye.

Then, as I walked in, I smiled to think I might lie down in my place and surprise them in the morning. Doing so, I heard a shrill cry that chilled my heart.

"Pieces of eight, pieces of eight!" the voice repeated. It was Silver's parrot, Captain Flint! He was the watch, and had found me out. I turned and heard Silver's familiar voice—

"Who goes?"

I turned, only to run into one body, then into another.

"Bring us some light, Dick," said Silver, when I was captured. A man left and soon returned with a flaming torch.

CHAPTER 21

In the Enemy's Camp

In the red glow of the torch, I knew all was lost. I saw only six pirates but they had taken the house. I assumed my friends were dead. The parrot sat on John's shoulder, and Silver turned to me. I could see that one of the men was wounded and the other four were barely awake. Only Silver seemed sharp, if pale.

"Well now," he said, "shiver me timbers. What a pleasant surprise. It's Jim Hawkins. Now, aren't you a smart lad."

I stood and watched him, saying nothing.

"Well, I always wanted you to join and now you will. You'll be one of us. Your friends don't want you anymore, it seems."

I knew then that they were alive—my heart gained hope but I said nothing.

"Well now, you can join or you can feel free to answer no. Now, that's right and fair, wouldn't you say?"

I felt the threat of death hanging over me but decided that now was my last chance to speak.

"If I'm to choose, I need to know what's what!"

"What's what," said Silver, "is that your friends have abandoned you. They woke to see the ship gone and came to see us and make terms. We took the stores and house and they took their leave. They're off to who-knows-where. But they said they'd had enough of you and that you had deserted them."

"Well," I said, "here's what's what with me.

You're in a bad way and it was me who put you there. I heard you from the apple barrel and spoiled your mutiny. I put Hands at the bottom of the sea. I cut the ship's cable and hid the ship where you'll never find it. Kill me if you wish. Or keep me alive and, if you do, I'll be a witness against you when you're in court for piracy. It's your choice!"

At this, one of the men stood with knife in hand, but Silver turned on him.

"Oh, are you Captain now? Think again, or I'll teach you better. Next man crosses me, he'll feed the fishes."

A few of the men rose up and argued but Silver put on his terrible face and wielded his cane.

"Do any want to challenge me?" he roared. "No, I thought not. Well, hold your tongues then. This boy is a braver man than the heap of you."

Now one of the men came forward, claiming

the crew's right to step outside and have a council without their Captain. This they did, leaving Silver and me alone. He looked at me and his eyes told me that he feared the worst.

"They'll turn on me, Jim. It's up to you and me to save each other."

I reacted with shock and squinted.

"I know you've got a ship somewhere. I don't know how, but I know it's so. Now, here's the question. Why did the doctor give me the map to the treasure before he left?"

Again I was amazed.

"Ah," said Silver, "that he did, but something is behind it, good or bad, Jim. That is the question."

CHAPTER 22

The Black Spot Returns

We then waited for the council to return, and when it did, Silver was friendly and familiar.

"Nice breeze, Jim," he said, and I watched him before turning my eye to the men outside.

When they returned, they came slowly, looking desperate and mean.

"Come on, I won't bite you," said Silver, "hand it over."

And with that, they gave him the Black Spot.

"Why, you've cut this out of a Bible. Now you're cursed!"

That said, they turned on each other and began to fight. He turned the spot over and read the word *"Deposed,"* which meant he was no longer to be called Captain.

But first, Silver insisted they read off his charges.

"You've made a mess of this cruise," said George Merry, "and you let the enemy out of this trap. Third, you wouldn't let us chase after them, and fourth, there's this boy."

"Well now," said Silver, "it's clear to me who wants to be Captain. But let me answer your charges. I made a mess of this cruise, did I? Well, you know what I wanted but you led them against me, didn't you, George? Who crossed me?"

With this, George looked away.

"You dare to accuse me! Trying to be Captain over me! You, that sank us all! You're not even a real pirate; you'd have done better as a tailor! And you have no idea how badly off we are right now. As for the boy, he's our hostage. I'm not going to kill our only hostage. He might be our last chance. And as for the deal I made, you would have done the same! Part of it is that the doctor returns each day to tend your wounds. And there's more. I've got something that will tell you why!"

With that, he dropped the treasure map on the floor and they all fell on it, crying and shouting like children. They behaved as if they had already found the gold and taken it home safe.

"Now, it was I found the treasure. Who's a better man than that? But I resign! Elect whoever you want! I'm done with it!"

But the three chanted "Silver, Silver, Silver" as George looked on. It was clear he was still Captain. Dick looked nervous about having cut his Bible. Silver turned it over in his hands and tossed it to me. I have it still.

"Well, George," said Silver, "looks like you'll have to wait to be Captain."

And with that, he sent George out on lookout while the crew and I turned to sleeping. I saw that we were nearing the end of this terrible game. I could not see what would become of us. I could not see why my friends had given Silver the map.

But I knew that he would do all in his power to save his miserable life. My heart was sore for him, for though he was evil, anyone could see that only darkness awaited him.

CHAPTER 23

On Parole

⌐∽

We were all wakened by the doctor's arrival and, I admit, I was ashamed to look him in the face.

When he came, Silver was bright and merry with him.

"Hallo Doctor! Top o' the morning to you, sir!" he cried. "Your patients are all doing well. Come and see."

He carried on like this as the doctor came up the hill.

"And we have a small surprise of a little stranger in our camp!"

With this, the doctor stopped.

"Not Jim!"

"Why, of course!" said Silver.

With this, the doctor looked shocked but insisted on examining his patients before turning his attention to me.

"I consider it my duty, as mutineers' doctor, to keep you all healthy enough to hang when we return to England."

After he had attended to the various ills of the pirates, he asked to speak to me alone. Again, the men protested and Silver turned on them.

"Silence!" he roared, like a lion. They all cowered before him. "Now, Doctor, we're all grateful for your help with our ills. Hawkins, will you give your word that you won't run away?"

This I did. Silver then asked the doctor to walk away down the hill and he would walk me out. Once the doctor was gone, the men turned to barking and yelling until Silver quieted them down.

"Do you want me to break our truce on the very day we go to look for the treasure? You fools! Dolts! We'll break it when it's our time."

And with this, he walked me out the door, where we made our way toward the doctor. Once there, his face changed entirely.

"Now, Doctor, I have saved this boy's life and I am now only here to save mine. I can only hope you'll assist us in both cases."

"Why, John," said the doctor, "you're not afraid?"

John admitted that he was and said he was bound to hang. But he hoped that the doctor would remember he had done some good in saving me.

With that, Silver left me with the doctor, who first scolded me until he heard my incredible story.

"You've found the ship?" he asked. "Why, it's been you all along who's been saving us, Jim."

And with that, he tried to encourage me to

break my word and come with him. But I wouldn't do it. I had given an oath. And so, he turned his attention to Silver.

"A word of advice: don't try to find that treasure."

"I have to," answered Silver, "or they will kill me themselves."

"Well," said the doctor, "then I warn you to beware of high winds at sea—those squalls can be deadly. And when we return, if we get out of this adventure alive, I pledge to do everything I can to save you."

With that, Silver beamed with joy and thanks. The doctor then shook my hand and took his leave of us at a brisk pace.

CHAPTER 24

The Treasure Hunt—Flint's Pointer

⌒

J im," said Silver, "if I saved your life, you've saved mine. I saw how the doctor asked you to run—you didn't and that saved me. Now look, I don't like this business. I don't know what the doctor meant about the squalls and I don't like our hunt today. Let's stick close."

With that, we returned to breakfast, where once again Silver's manner changed. He became loud and boastful and said that the doctor had told him the ship was hidden. He made wild plans that they would soon have the treasure and be on the high seas, with me as hostage.

The men laughed and seemed ready for anything. I knew that Silver still had his foot in both camps. And I worried that his crew should find out his new loyalty to the doctor and that he and I would have to fight them off. It would be a sore sight. He with one leg and me, a boy, against five powerful pirates.

Also, I worried that I could not make out the actions of my friends. Why had they left the fort and given up the map? And what was the warning of the squalls about? I had many doubts in my mind as we set out on our journey.

Each man wore several weapons, and Silver led the sorry party with two rifles, two pistols, a cutlass sword, and Captain Flint on his shoulder, jabbering. We made a fine picture as we headed out.

As we followed the directions, we looked to the chart and the men argued over which tall tree at the point might be the one mentioned on the map. Each picked his favorite, and Silver told them we'd soon enough know who was right when we arrived.

We walked on easily and then, bending to our left, went up a crest. We now moved into denser jungle and suddenly, we heard one of the crew's voice rise in terror. We all went up to him as a group and found him staring down at the skeleton of a man lying by a tree.

"What way is that for bones to lie?" asked Silver. "It ain't natural." With that we all looked at the skeleton and saw that it was laid out straight, which seemed odd. Then Silver pulled out his compass. He took a bearing along the straight line of the bones and shook his head.

"I thought so. This here's a pointer. This is a

jolly joke of Flint's. This is one of the men he killed. Why, look at his hair, that would be Allardyce. You remember him, Tom?"

"Aye, aye," Tom answered, "he owed me money."

"I never liked that Flint," answered another man, "the way he raged and cursed and sang only that one song. He carried the jinx . . ."

"Come now," said Silver, "enough of that kind of talk. Think ahead to the treasure and let's move!"

We did so, but the men walked more closely and quietly. Gone was their carefree talk. The seaman's bones and Flint's terrifying pointer had made their spirits fall.

CHAPTER 25

The Voice Among the Trees

⌒

The men were now exhausted and rattled and sat down at the first opportunity. They all turned to talk of Flint.

"He was so ugly. And his temper was vicious."

"Well then," said Silver, "you should thank your stars he's dead." Then, all at once, we heard a voice call out:

"Fifteen men on a dead man's chest—
Yo-ho-ho, and a bottle of rum!"

The men were instantly in terror.

"It's Flint!" they cried, "back from the dead!"

And then, the voice called out, "Fetch me my sword, Darby!"

"Those were his last words!" one of the men cried out.

The pirates stayed rooted to the ground, each man crying that he wanted to go and that they were afraid of ghosts. Dick, who was the man with fever and sickness in the group, read from his Bible and seemed about to go mad. But Silver stood his ground.

"That voice had an echo!" he said. "Ghosts don't have echocs! That's someone made of flesh and blood!"

This seemed to bring the men around.

"Aye," said one, "that didn't sound like Flint, it sounded like someone else. It sounded like Ben Gunn!"

And it was clear none was afraid of Ben Gunn, even if they thought him dead. Even as a ghost, they were not concerned about him. Soon the men were back on track and turning their attention toward the climb ahead. Silver pulled me by the rope with which they had tied my hands, and I could see his mood change. I could tell his mind was on the treasure. He scowled my way as he pulled me along. I knew then that all thought of mercy was gone from him. He would try to find the treasure and his ship and slit the throat of any man who stood in his way.

I was shaken and tired and Dick continued to babble madly behind as we walked in the blazing heat. I thought of the many men who had been killed here by Flint and thought I would be next.

Suddenly, we were in the clearing and heard Merry shouting out as we moved forward. We ran to him and Silver doubled his pace until we all came to a halt.

Before us was a great hole, and we could tell that it was not new. The sides were caved in and grass had grown in it. At its bottom were a broken pick and bits of packing crate from the *Walrus*, Flint's ship. But all was clear, too. The hoard had been found and raided and the seven hundred thousand pounds of treasure were gone!

∽

Now the men were in a rage. They all yelled out and cursed, but with Silver, the change was quicker. He turned and handed me a pistol and we quickly stepped off to the side.

"So," I said, "you've changed sides again?"

He paid me no mind, and the men jumped in the pit to find only one single coin. They nimbly climbed out and turned to Silver, their eyes spelling murder.

"So this is the wooden-legged fool who's led

us here!" said George Merry. "Well, look at his face. He knew all along there was no treasure."

They all glared at Silver, who soon spoke up. "So, back to seeking the post of Captain, eh, George?"

They stood across from us and we looked toward them, pistols ready.

"There's two of them, one a cripple and one a boy, whose heart I will have—and there's five of us," said George.

But just then, shots rang out and two of the men dropped, with Merry falling into the pit. Long John quickly fired both rounds into him and said, "I reckon I settled you, George."

Suddenly, the doctor, Gray, and Ben Gunn joined us with their smoking pistols. We ran quickly through the woods to cut off the escaped men from the boats. Soon enough, we found they had gone in the wrong direction—we took a rest while the doctor explained what had happened.

Ben, in his yearlong wanderings, had found the skeleton and the treasure. He had dug up the gold and transported it to his cave only two months before we arrived on the island. It was the afternoon of the attack when the doctor had gotten this confession from him. The next morning, after seeing the boat gone, the doctor had gone to Silver and given him the map. After all, it was useless now. And he had given him the supplies in order to gain our friends safe passage to Ben's cave, where there was salted goat in great supply. He also wished to keep the treasure secure.

That morning, they had headed back to cut us off, knowing that we would seek the treasure. Ben had run ahead and, remembering his shipmates' superstitions, had called out and frightened them.

"Lucky I had Hawkins," said Silver, "or no one had come for me."

Everyone agreed with him, and we made our

way off around the point to the boats. We then paddled by the mouth of Ben's cave and saw the Squire waving to us. We also saw the *Hispaniola* floating offshore, raised by the oncoming tides.

We pulled into the cove, and there the Squire scowled and cursed Silver, but let him be. Then all entered the cove and saw Captain Smollett resting beside a fire and great heaps of gold and treasure. So many had died to find it, and so many had died to claim it. Ships and bodies lay at the bottom of the sea on account of it.

"I don't think we'll go to sea again, shall we, Jim?" said the doctor.

And with that, we fell to eating a delicious meal with food gathered from the boat. Silver sat back and seemed again to be the man who had first appeared to me: helpful, quiet, and courteous. The perfect seaman.

CHAPTER 26

A Fond Farewell—We Make
Our Way Home

⁓

We spent the next days carrying our vast treasure into the boats and then onto the *Hispaniola*.
As I was too young to do the work of the stronger
men, I was given the task of filling canvas sacks
with the treasure so that the others could carry it
away. One by one, I filled each bag with the pre-
cious stuff, sealing them at the top with a large
sailor's needle and thread. It was long, hard work,
but worth the effort. We worried about the three
remaining pirates, but thankfully, heard little
of them.

The treasure was a collection of coins from around the world. Until that moment, I had had no idea that money came in such a variety of forms and styles. Along with the French and English coins I had seen before, there were piles of Spanish doubloons and Venetian ducats. Even stranger were the square coins with holes in the middle from faraway China that perhaps Marco Polo had come across on his journeys. I sifted through them, letting them fall like autumn leaves through my fingers.

One night, we heard the raving of the mutineers. For our part, Silver had been treated civilly, but kept at a distance, like a dog leashed to a post. No man would hear him out, for although he played kind, we knew he was not to be trusted.

We decided we must maroon the mutineers—there was no point in bringing them home to hang. So we loaded Ben's cave with a good stock of sail, as well as tools, food, and other supplies. Then we readied our ship.

As we were leaving, we passed by the three men in the shallows we could still make out ashore, begging us to take them along. We hailed them, and the doctor told them of the small stores of food we had left. Still they begged, and, when it was clear we would not stop, they fired on us and just missed Silver himself.

Soon the craggy peaks were fading from view and I felt a great joy to be leaving Treasure Island behind me. We were short of men and each had to do his part. The Captain still needed rest and was giving his orders from a cot on deck.

In time we reached Spanish America and greeted the people there with great joy. We tasted their fruits and vegetables, and the Captain found another English shipmaster with whom he was invited to spend the evening telling of our adventures. When we returned to the *Hispaniola*, we found Ben Gunn alone on deck telling us that Silver had taken a small craft and some small sacks of treasure and had made off. I think we all felt relieved when we knew he had gone for good.

To make a long story short, we got a few good hands on board there, and made our way home just before a search party was sent to rescue us. We all got a fair share of the treasure, and spent it in various ways.

Gray saved his money, gained an education, and got married. He is now a part owner of a full-rigged ship. Ben Gunn lost his one thousand pounds within three weeks and was back begging on the fourth. Our good Captain retired.

Of Silver, we heard no more. I imagine he located his wife and is still living with his parrot Captain Flint. As for me, though there may still be gold on Treasure Island, I shall never return. When I have bad dreams, they are of the booming surf and of the sharp voice of Captain Flint ringing in my ears: "Pieces of eight! Pieces of eight!"

What Do *You* Think?

Questions for Discussion

⟡

Have you ever been around a toddler who keeps asking the question "Why?" Does your teacher call on you in class with questions from your homework? Do your parents ask you questions at the dinner table about your day? We are always surrounded by questions that need a specific response. But is it possible to have a question with no right answer?

The following questions are about the book you just read. But this is not a quiz! They are designed to help you look at the people, places, and events in the story from different angles. These questions do not have specific answers. Instead, they might make you think of the story in a completely new way.

Think carefully about each question and enjoy discovering more about this classic story.

1. At the beginning of the book, Jim is about to embark on an incredible adventure. How would you feel starting out on a journey all by yourself? Where would you go?

2. Would you leave your friends and family if it meant you might find treasure?

3. In chapter 4, Jim describes hearing footsteps and seeing visions appear in the mist. How did reading about Jim's fear make you feel? Did you get a sense that something scary was about to happen?

4. Why did Jim cry when he realized that a new apprentice had been sent to the inn? Have you ever felt this way?

5. John Silver is an unusual character. He is likable one minute and treacherous the next. Have you ever met someone like that?

6. When Jim is in the apple barrel, he overhears John Silver's plan to kill the Captain. What would you have done? Have you ever overheard something you were not supposed to hear?

7. When Jim decided to hide himself in one of the boats, he said, "It was then that I became either brave or stupid, I can't say which." What do you think? What would you have done if you were Jim?

8. Ben tells Jim, "I have nothing, but I am rich." What do you think he meant by that?

9. Throughout the book, the only woman we see is Jim's mother. Why do you think this is? Could women today go on such adventures?

10. There are a lot of unusual pirate-like terms used in the book. One of these is "Flint's Fist." What do you think that means? Try creating other pirate terms to describe things.

Afterword

by Arthur Pober, EdD

⌒℘

First impressions are important.

Whether we are meeting new people, going to new places, or picking up a book unknown to us, first impressions count for a lot. They can lead to warm, lasting memories or can make us shy away from any future encounters.

Can you recall your own first impressions and earliest memories of reading the classics?

Do you remember wading through pages and pages of text to prepare for an exam? Or were you the child who hid under the blanket to read with a flashlight, joining forces with Robin Hood to save Maid Marian? Do you remember only how long it took you to read a lengthy novel such as *Little Women*? Or did you become best friends with the March sisters?

Even for a gifted young reader, getting through long chapters with dense language can easily become overwhelming and can obscure the richness of the story and its characters. Reading an abridged, newly crafted version of a classic novel can be the gentle introduction a child needs to explore the characters and story line without the frustration of difficult vocabulary and complex themes.

Reading an abridged version of a classic novel gives the young reader a sense of independence and the satisfaction of finishing a "grown-up" book. And when a child is engaged with and inspired by a classic story, the tone is set for further exploration of the story's themes, characters, history, and details. As a child's reading skills advance, the desire to tackle the original, unabridged version of the story will naturally emerge.

If made accessible to young readers, these stories can become invaluable tools for understanding themselves in the context of their families and social environments. This is why the Classic Starts series includes questions that stimulate discussion regarding the impact and social relevance of the characters and stories today. These questions can foster lively conversations between children and their parents or teachers. When we look at the issues, values, and standards of past times in terms of how we live now, we can appreciate literature's classic tales in a very personal and engaging way.

Share your love of reading the classics with a young child, and introduce an imaginary world real enough to last a lifetime.

Dr. Arthur Pober, EdD

Dr. Arthur Pober has spent more than twenty years in the fields of early-childhood and gifted education. He is the former principal of one of the world's oldest laboratory schools for gifted youngsters, Hunter College Elementary School, and former director of Magnet Schools for the Gifted and Talented for more than 25,000 youngsters in New York City.

Dr. Pober is a recognized authority in the areas of media and child protection and is currently the U.S. representative to the European Institute for the Media and European Advertising Standards Alliance.

Explore these wonderful stories in our
Classic Starts® library

20,000 Leagues Under the Sea

The Adventures of Huckleberry Finn

The Adventures of Robin Hood

The Adventures of Sherlock Holmes

The Adventures of Tom Sawyer

Alice in Wonderland & Through the Looking-Glass

Animal Stories

Anne of Avonlea

Anne of Green Gables

Arabian Nights

Around the World in 80 Days

Ballet Stories

Black Beauty

The Call of the Wild

Dracula

Five Little Peppers and How They Grew

Frankenstein

Great Expectations

Greek Myths

Grimm's Fairy Tales

Gulliver's Travels

Heidi

The Hunchback of Notre-Dame

The Iliad

Journey to the Center of the Earth

The Jungle Book

The Last of the Mohicans

Little Lord Fauntleroy

Little Men

A Little Princess

Little Women

The Man in the Iron Mask

Moby-Dick

The Odyssey

Oliver Twist

Peter Pan